Disney's
KiM POSSIBLE

THE KiM POSSIBLE FILES

By Rich Mintzer

Based on the series
created by

**Mark McCorkle
& Bob Schooley**

Disney PRESS

VOLO
New York

W9-CTA-208

Copyright © 2003 Disney Enterprises, Inc.
All rights reserved. No part of this book may be reproduced or transmitted in any form or by any means,
electronic or mechanical, including photocopying, recording, or by any information storage and retrieval system,
without permission from the publisher. For information address
Disney Press, 114 Fifth Avenue, New York, New York 10011–5690.
Printed in the United States of America
First Edition
1 3 5 7 9 10 8 6 4 2
Library of Congress Catalog Card Number on file
ISBN 0-7868-4572-4
For more Disney Press fun, visit www.disneybooks.com
Visit Kim every day at DisneyChannel.com

What's the sitch?

I certainly didn't plan to become a teen hero—it just sort of . . . happened. When I first created my Website, I put up an ad saying I could do anything. I meant typical stuff like baby-sitting, walking dogs, running errands, mowing lawns, washing cars, that kind of thing. But wouldn't you know, people started asking me for help retrieving stolen secret formulas, tracking down missing plans for nuclear reactors, and stopping mad scientists from trying to take over the world. Well, how could I say no?

So that's how it all started.

I've put together a bunch of memories—lots of photos, newspaper headlines, and even a few letters and e-mails from the past year—since I've become a crime fighter. I even wrote about some of my coolest adventures. I think this book really rocks. Hope you like it, too!

Later, K.P.

First, a little about my normal life . . .

I'm your basic, average, high-school student who's trying to save the world in her spare time. That may sound like a lot, but what it comes right down to is that I'm a high school sophomore, captain of the junior varsity cheerleading team, and also an international crime fighter. I do homework, take pop quizzes, and hang out with my best friend, like everyone else.

I just make the headlines in the local newspaper a lot more often than any of my classmates.

To my best friend Kim,

Ron

My best friend is Ron Stoppable. He's a great guy who never has any trouble sticking by me through any of the messes I get in. Okay, so he complains a lot when we're on a mission together, but he's still a great guy and my best friend.

Bueno Nacho

Our favorite hangout is Bueno Nacho—the local fast-food joint. We spend so much time there because our school cafeteria food is, well, pretty much untouchable.

...eton High—Lunch Menu OCTOBER

Check out this month's menu!

MONDAY	TUESDAY	WEDNESDAY	THURSDAY	FRIDAY
		1 Creamed herring on toast / Radish salad / Prune cake	**2** Leek casserole / Tuna soup / Prune whip	**3** Tofu-chunks chili / Refried beets / Prune-apple pie
...tery Meat ...nday! (...entify the meat, ...t a free barley- ...une cookie!) ...snip salad	**7** Chipped beef à la Gertrude / Pork rind soup / Prune ice cream	**8** Cod pot pie / Asparagus chips / Prune fritters	**9** Pork croquettes / Creamed corn / Prune yogurt	**10** Spinach linguine with tuna balls / Oatmeal-raisin soup / Prune biscotti
...stery Meat Monday! (...identify the meat, ...get a free barley- prune cookie!) ...eek chips	**14** Tuna-noodle casserole / Mushroom chips / Prune pudding	**15** Spaghetti with beetballs / Artichoke puffs / Prune brownie	**16** Turkey loaf with pineapple glaze / Asparagus salad / Prune cobbler	**17** Fish pizza / Yogurt soup / Prune cheesecake
...0 Mystery Meat Monday! (identify the meat, get a free barley- prune cookie!) Liver & onion soup	**21** Kidney bean taco / Refried beets / Prune flan	**22** Radish sandwich / Succotash salad / Prune torte	**23** Boiled chicken / Radish salad / Prune gelatin	**24** Tuna patties with pineapple glaze / Kidney bean soup / Prune custard
27 Mystery Meat Monday! (identify the meat, get a free barley- prune cookie!) Jalapeño salad	**28** Pumpkin surprise / Salmon puffs / Prune pie	**29** Turkey loaf with tomato sauce / Parsnip chips / Prune parfait	**30** Spaghetti with beetballs / Artichoke puffs / Prune mousse	**31 Happy Halloween!** "Dracula's" blood sausage / "Ghoulish" goulash / "Terrifying" prune tart

A Typical Day at Middleton High

CLASS SCHEDULE

8:00–8:55	Geometry
9:00–9:55	Introduction to Chemistry
10:00–10:55	Computer Science
11:00–11:55	Environmental Sciences
12:00–12:55	Lunch
1:00–1:55	English Composition
2:00–2:55	Monday & Wednesday: Gym

Tuesday	Introduction to Advanced Laser Technology
Thursday	Political Science
Friday	Abnormal Psychology

Aside from the food, our high school is pretty okay. There's always lots to do—like make a fool of myself in front of my crush, Josh Mankey; get detention for being late to class (again); and the regularly scheduled stuff, too.

After-school Activities:

Monday: Cheerleading practice

Tuesday: Cheerleading practice

Wednesday: Cheerleading practice

Thursday: Cheerleading practice

Friday: Shopping at Club Banana!

THIS WEEK'S EVENTS:

SPIRIT WEEK—Let's show that Mad Dog spirit all week long

DANCE FRIDAY—Sadie Hawkins-style—girls ask the guys.

CHEERLEADING TRYOUTS—Help lead the Mad Dogs to VIC-TOR-Y!

(Maybe someday I'll get up the courage to ask Josh to a dance.)

That's it, for now. I'm sure I'll have many more exciting adventures as I save the world in my spare time. I'll keep my fingers crossed that I don't embarrass myself too much, (especially when Josh is nearby!) and that the villains keep their evil plans to a minimum!

Later!

Love, Kim

. . . My Most Embarrassing Moment

Bonnie Rockwaller invited my folks to be the chaperones at the school ski trip. Thanks, Bon.

The 'rents spent most of the day embarrassing me, except when they took a break to totally humiliate me. It was so not fun! But, believe it or not, in the end it turned out okay. My dad helped rescue Ron, Rufus, Mr. Barkin and me from an avalanche on his motorized snowboard. He totally rocked! Even better, Bonnie's mom showed up, which was so cool 'cause we learned that her nickname is Bon-Bon! That so made up for all my embarrassment!

Runner-up: Most Embarrassing Moment #2

Yes, that's me accidentally ripping down the banner Josh Mankey made for the school dance. It was a total accident, but that doesn't make me look any cooler.

That's my school, Middleton High.

This is my good friend Monique. She's not a crime fighter. Not that she's against it, but it's just not her thing. Monique keeps me up on all the important stuff going on at school, like who's wearing what, what's the latest gossip, and what the fashion du jour is.

That's me with Rufus.
(Ron took the picture, which explains the thumbprint.)

Me again

More Middleton High

I've got the latest in high-tech lockers, complete with computer, laser printer, scanner, and gym shorts.

That's the cafeteria. That blob on a plate is supposed to be food. The jury is still out on what it really is.

That's the seniors' table. They totally think they run the school . . . well, actually, they do.

That's me with Josh Mankey at the dance. He's so totally cute.

Can you believe I got detention? The 'rents were more tweaked about that than when I go off to fight some mad scientist halfway around the world.

The Great Shopping Debate, Club Banana vs. Smarty Mart

He may be my best friend, but Ron does have his faults, one of which is shopping at Smarty Mart. He loves their bargain basement junk! Of course, he calls me a retail snob 'cause I shop at Club Banana.

What I like About . . .
Club Banana by Kim   Smarty Mart by Ron

Trendy jeans . . . . Same jeans as Club Banana for, like, 1/10 the price

So not the same . . . . Are, too

Are not! . . . . Are, too!

Really cool leather jackets . . . . 100 percent synthetic mock-leather jackets

Great selection of sweaters! . . . . Slightly irregular sweaters (3 sleeves)
                                              —10 for $15! Can't beat that!

Designer brands! . . . . Canned meats!

The coolest accessories . . . . Practical stuff like glow-in-the-dark toilet seats

Friendly staff helps you . . . . Friendly staff helps you cram more bargain
                                              stuff into your cart

Designer boots for under $90 . . . . Find two boots that match—only $7 a pair

Clothes people will notice! . . . . Clothes pets can chew on!

Ron and me dealing with some of Drakken's henchmen

That's Bonnie climbing out of a Dumpster. I just had to throw that one in here.

This is what we get for dealing with the world's cheapest crook.

Middleton High School

Report Card: <u>First semester</u>   Name: <u>**Kimberly Ann Possible**</u>

Course	Grade	Teacher Comments
Geometry	B	Kim needs to spend more time with theorems and less time talking with that Wade fellow on that fancy walkie-talkie of hers.
Chemistry	A	Kim prevents more explosions then she causes, which is a big plus for the other students!
Computer Science	A	Kimberly is a whiz on the computer. Her use of computers in saving the planet is really paying off.
Environmental Sciences	A+	Kim's eco-awareness is excellent! She exhibits a true concern for the environment—she even risked her life to save a manatee.
English Composition	B	I think Kim is quite capable. She does, however, need to stop using words like "sitch" and phrases like "no big" in serious compositions.
Gym	A+	Kim has remarkable athletic skills. She can tumble and twirl better than anyone I know.
Advanced Laser Tech.	A	Kimberly truly has a grasp of lasers and how to use them effectively.
Political Science	A+	Her world travels and keen understanding of the subject serve her well in this area.
Abnormal Psychology	A	Kim has a rich and thorough understanding of the abnormal mind—like all the villains she deals with.

Parent's Signature

Dr. Possible

_____

I'm not a bad student at all. In fact, I get pretty good grades. It's awfully hard trying to find the time to fit in cheerleading practice, homework, and fighting evil, but I do my best. I mean, if I can survive high school, I can probably save the world, too, right?

> From: A Very Secret Scientist
> To: Possible, Kim
> Subject: Your Ad
>
Hi, Kim:
I'm a top-level scientist working on a secret formula at a secret location in a secret province of a secret country. My secret formula has been stolen from the secret safe. Is there any chance you might have some time to help me find it? Of course, you can't tell anyone that you've come here, met me, or found the formula . . . if you find it. Please let me know if you're up to the secret challenge.

Regards,
A Very Secret Scientist

Something told me that I was in for something unusual. . . .

You can't imagine how many mornings start off like a typical school day. I'm having breakfast, thinking about how I can convince the 'rents to let me get some cool jeans from Club Banana. Then next thing I know, I'm being whisked off to some other part of the world, chasing a badly dressed, evil billionaire, who has some really warped plan to take over the world.

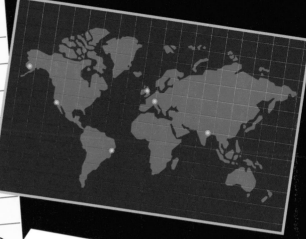

A few of the places I've been in my pursuit of criminals

Tropical Rain Forest

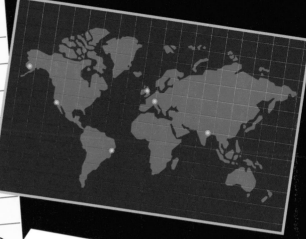
Monkey Temple Ruins

France

Swiss Alps

The Jungle

Island Lab

GO, MAD DOGS!

When I'm not chasing evil villains around the world, I usually can be found at cheerleading practice.

That's the cheerleading squad, minus Bonnie, who got me really tweaked one day by saying something about my moves being passé, so I ripped her out of the photo. She's so not the ego booster.

My Likes: Shopping at Club Banana, cheerleading, hanging with my friends Ron and Monique, saving the world from evil villains

My Dislikes: Supervillains with bad breath, being dissed by Bonnie Rockwaller, Smarty Mart, baby-sitting my twin brothers

This is a photo of me at home with my brain-surgeon mom, rocket-scientist dad, and terrible tweeb* twin brothers Jim & Tim. Pretty much your typical family—but way too much brainpower going on.

Never try explaining to a rocket scientist why you want to buy a really cool pair of boots—when you already have a pair of boots, but they are so last year. He'll give you the chemical breakdown of what makes something cool, as in low temperature.

*Definition: Dweeb twins squared = Tweeb!

Jim & Tim Possible
(aka Tweeb Brothers)

Note: When I said I could do anything, it did not include baby-sitting the twins. I'd prefer being locked in combat with Shego. And she has claws that shoot out some pretty painful rays. But more about her later.

Likes: Inventing stuff, rock-ets, blowing things up, busting into my room, driving me crazy. Blowing more stuff up!

Dislikes: Acting normal!

Ron Stoppable

That's me and Ron Stoppable, my best pal and sidekick. Don't get any ideas—Ron and I are just friends. We met way back on the first day of preschool. His pants fell down, and he tripped over them, so I caught him. He always comes with me on my missions, and I still have to save him a lot of the time. Ron's pants still do fall down with some regularity, but I don't need to catch him anymore. Not much, anyway.

Ron has some pretty strange ideas. Back when we worked at Bueno Nacho for a very brief period of time, Ron worked his way up to management by coming up with his combination of nacho and taco, or as he calls it, the "naco." That was definitely way better than his previous idea to combine a squash with a knish, which he called a squanish.

I give you . . . the naco.

What can I say, we've shared a sandbox, played hide-and-seek, gone trick-or-treating, attended the first day of high school together, and battled notorious evil villains in far corners of the world . . . just your typical best-friend stuff.

Happy Halloween!

Hang on, Ron!

Not-so-happy camper

Likes: Rufus (pet naked mole rat), bargain hunting (so not my thing), helping me save the world, nacos

Dislikes: Climbing (actually the falling and getting hurt part), bugs, poison ivy, and anything else that reminds him of Camp Wannaweep (which was where he went as a child and was tortured by bugs, slimy food, and a toxic swimming hole)

Biggest fears: Getting a really bad haircut; Rufus running off to join the circus

Ron and I have been friends for so long that I feel like we speak our own language. Although as you can see from the list below, we don't *always* have the same things to say:

ME:

So not the drama .... Wow-chow!

What's the sitch? .... Bon diggity

Tell me something I don't know .... Fantabulous

No big .... It's all gravy, baby.

Thanks for the lift .... Badical!

RON:

RUFUS

Ron keeps his buddy Rufus in his pocket. Rufus has come in handy a few times when we were off saving the world. But, for the most part, I wish Ron would keep the little rat at home—especially when we go out for food. Rodents and food just do not mix.

Ron's pocket protector

May I take your order?

Likes: Sleeping in Ron's pocket, swimming in melted cheese, food, being naked

Dislikes: Restaurants and stores with strict "no pet" policies

Biggest fear: Getting tossed in the washing machine when Ron's mom cleans his clothes

Hairless rodents do not amuse me.

WADE

This is Wade. He's got to be the smartest kid in the world. He's a ten-year-old computer genius who can find out everything about anyone (and anything) with just a few taps on his computer—even the password to my diary (I keep changing it, but he's way too smart!). Wade is always ready to help us find whatever info we need. He rocks!

Don't know what I'll do if Wade ever gets an off-line social life. The world would suffer, for sure.

Likes: Computers, connector cables, hi-tech toys, soda, snacks

Dislikes: Going outside, ever

Biggest fear: That his mom and dad will pull the plug on his computer time

Wade really takes great pride in having created the Holo-Kim, a life-sized, walking-talking hologram of me. How cool is that?! Great for being in two places at once, like at a party on a school night. Just kidding, Mom. Can you tell which is the real me?

I'm the one on the left. Or am I?

Great Gadgets
from the Creative Mind of Wade!

Okay, what self-respecting crime fighter doesn't have some really cool gadgets? Here are some of mine. Sorry, you can't order them from your favorite high-tech catalog.

Kimmunicator

I use it to talk to Wade from anywhere in the world. I'd be totally lost without it. It's a cross between a high-tech walkie-talkie and a video cell phone! (With free Long Distance on weekends, of course!)

Jetpack Backpack

When you really need to get out of a place in a hurry, this backpack really flies! Just be careful not to put too many textbooks in it or it'll slow you down.

Elastic Firing Lipstick

Shoots out elastic sticky goop, plus I really like this shade of pink!

Hair Dryer/Grappling Hook

Shoots out a hook line so I can swing out of danger. Also good for getting out of the detention room . . . not that I would know, of course.

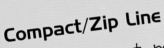

Compact/Zip Line

It's part compact, part zip line, and the mirror is perfect for reflecting laser beams or checking your makeup.

Scanner Sunglasses

Not only do they look cool but they can also emit a Day-Glo beam and scan in information. They even zoom in for close shots of whatever you're looking at. Good on a secret mission or if you want to check the label on someone's cool jeans.

VILLAINS

Wade keeps a file on the most dangerous criminals we've had to deal with. Some of them keep coming back again and again. They just never seem to learn.

DR. DRAKKEN

WANTED

DR. DRAKKEN

Job: Mad scientist
Distinguishing features: Blue skin, bad breath
Wanted for: Attempting to take over the world
Most dangerous weapon:
His childhood stories—hearing them could put anyone to sleep

That's Doctor Drakken—he's not really a doctor, just your basic mad-scientist type. He's got that blue skin, which is good because it makes him easy to spot in a crowd. And he wears a ponytail, which he thinks is cool. He's so very wrong.

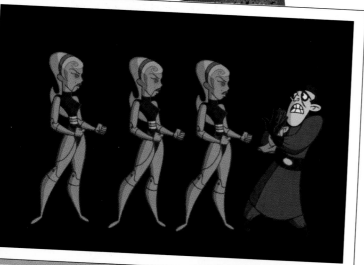

Drakken has his own brainless henchmen. They follow him around, either because they think he's going to give them good jobs when he takes over the world or because they really get a kick out of watching him make a fool of himself. Personally, I think it's the latter, because why else would these guys work for a nasty, foul-breathed boss? Unless he offers great benefits. You never know. . . .

Drakken's tried all sorts of dastardly plans. Once he tried to create a trio of evil robots, but even *they* didn't follow his lame plans.

He also loves barking orders, especially at Shego. No wonder she's so high-strung.

SHEGO

Shego works for Dr. Drakken, except for all the times she quits because his plans are beyond stupid and she doesn't want to be a part of them, like when he tried to clone her. I'd quit, too, if my boss wanted to clone me. Flattering, perhaps, but totally creepy! Even evil villains should know where to draw the line. Drakken is basically mad as in "mad scientist," and Shego just plain mad, as in really bad hair day—every day.

Shego does the fighting for Drakken, and she *is* pretty tough, I must admit. I think if she used her moves for good instead of evil, she could be a head cheerleader, no problem.

WANTED

SHEGO

Job: Evil sidekick
Distinguishing features: Green skin, ray-throwing claws
Wanted for: Attempted world domination
Most dangerous weapon: Her bad attitude

SEÑOR SENIOR, SR. & SEÑOR SENIOR, JR.

The biggest prob is that the Seniors have major money, so they can buy all the evil tools they need to wreak havoc around the globe. This cuts into my cheerleading practice schedule. It makes managing my time really tough. That's their island lair, above. With all that money, why couldn't they just take up shuffleboard and cruise around the world instead of doing the criminal thing?

WANTED

SEÑOR SENIOR, JR.

Job: Being a sinister multibillionaire's son
Distinguishing features:
Fake bake tan and Caesar haircut
Wanted for: Assisting in
attempt of controlling the world
Most dangerous weapon: His simple mind

WANTED

SEÑOR SENIOR, SR.

Job: Being a sinister multibillionaire
Distinguishing features:
Bad posture, unstylish suits
Wanted for: Attempted world domination
Most dangerous weapon:
Too much time on his hands

DNAMY

DNAmy's hard to miss. She's always wearing a stuffed otterfly and green gloves. The worst thing about Amy is that she likes to make mutated animals like a half-dog half-lobster—the only pet that can run and fetch its own butter sauce. As long as I can keep her away from her Genetic Zipper DNA Fusion Machine, she can't do too much harm (except to the fashion-conscious world).

WANTED

DNAMY

Job: Wicked biogeneticist
Distinguishing features: Glasses, gap in teeth
Wanted for: Engineering life-sized Cuddle Buddies
Most dangerous weapon:
Her passion for stuffed animals

DUFF KILLIGAN

Duff is probably the world's best-known rogue golfer . . . or perhaps the world's *only* rogue golfer. He's never won a major tournament—probably not a minor one, either. He loves golf so much that his goal is to make the world one giant golf course by covering it in grass. He's dangerous when he's got his golf clubs in his hand, especially because he likes to hit exploding golf balls. As Ron says, he doesn't worry about trying to get the ball into the hole . . . anywhere an exploding golf ball lands, there's a hole.

WANTED

DUFF KILLIGAN
Job: Rogue golfer
Distinguishing features: Red beard, green beret
Wanted for: Attempting to make the world one large golf course
Most dangerous weapon: His slice

KNIGHTS OF RODEGHAN

These guys must have stayed up late, watching too many King Arthur movies. I mean a bunch of knights in armor running around with lasers? That's wrong in so many ways! They came to fulfill some sort of prophecy and ended up making a mess of the Middleton Mini-Golf.

LORD MONTY FISKE/ MONKEY FIST

Fiske was a well-spoken, world-famous explorer and a highly respected scholar—until he went bonkers and decided to try very costly, dangerous, radical monkey genetic mutation upon himself. And unlike Tarzan, he's no fun-loving swinger. Instead, he's obsessed with monkey mystical power, (aka monkey kung fu). He can appear quite the cordial gentleman, but the monkey hands and feet give him away. He so needs a manicure, a pedicure, and perhaps a banana.

WANTED

KNIGHTS OF RODEGHAN

Job: Leading attack against King Wallace's son, Wally
Distinguishing features: Lots of armor, really shiny
Wanted for: Attempting to kill Prince Wallace III
Most dangerous weapon: Modern laser technology

WANTED

LORD MONTY FISKE

Job: English nobleman gone bad
Distinguishing features: Monkey hands and feet, martial arts attire
Wanted for: Attempting to gain mystical monkey power
Most dangerous weapon: His killer monkey moves

THE CHEESE WHEEL

Me telling Ron he is *not* the boss of me

Me and Shego. So not the good time.

Say "Cheese!"

I took an after-school job at Bueno Nacho and signed Ron up to work with me. Of course, friends don't always work well together. After Ron and I had a major fight, I quit to go off and stop Drakken from his latest attack. He had taken over Wisconsin's Cheese Wheel Mall and ordered Shego to drill into the earth's surface to reach magma that would flow out and melt the state. Unfortunately, just as I got there, Drakken captured me. When Ron found out, he left Bueno Nacho to rescue me. Of course, he got captured, too . . . but it's the thought that counts, right? We got free, and I fought Shego. Meanwhile, Ron flooded the place with cheese, and then Drakken and Shego were sent paddling up a cheesy river.

My Greatest Adventures

THE TWEEBS

Baby-sitting in a rain forest? No big.

We are so totally _not_ holding hands.

Check it, Mom—the twins only _look_ innocent!

There I was, baby-sitting the tweebs (my twin brothers, Tim & Jim—the Im-Possible pair), and the next thing I know, I'm taking my brothers along on a visit to Drakken's secret lair in the Peruvian Rain Forest. Drakken and Shego had swiped some sort of mind-control chip, and I had to get it back. Then Drakken captures me, and suddenly I'm under his control. That's when it all got blurry. Ron tells me that Shego and I tried to capture Ron! Finally, believe it or not, the tweebs saved the day with their handheld silicon phase disrupter (and I thought they were carrying around a video game), which disabled Drakken's mind-control chip. Of course, I tried to use the mind-control thing to get the twins to behave, but Mom caught on. Can't blame a big sister for trying.

THE NANO TICK

Shark bait

Nacho showdown—Shego throw-down!

Ron and I went to Drakken's island hideout to get back a stolen microbug called a nano-tick. Of course, Drakken captured us and tossed us into a shark tank. Thanks to a spray of my elastic firing lipstick, we escaped. No big, right? Wrong. When we got back to school, I had this exploding nano-tick stuck to my nose. It looked like a big zit! And, even worse, I got detention for being late to class. I used my cheerleading moves to bolt from detention and escape to Bueno Nacho.

But Shego and Drakken caught up to me. Thanks to some help from my new detention buddies, I was able to get Shego out of the way. Then Ron poured some Diablo sauce (the very hot and spicy stuff) on me. It took care of the tick, and then I used the tick to take care of Drakken.

Ron's Diablo de-ticking sauce

My Greatest Adventures

THE ROGUE GOLFER

Agent Will Du (Can you say smug?)

A golfer with one nasty slice

One time, I got to work with the Global Justice Network, and I even showed up their big-shot agent Will Du. We tracked down a missing scientist who had invented superfast-growing grass. Sure enough, the formula ended up in the hands of Duff Killigan, the rogue golfer. He wanted to cover the whole world in grass and make it into one large golf course. I had to escape a quicksand trap and dodge exploding golf balls before I finally captured Killigan. And that arrogant agent Will Du only thanked me for assisting him! *Assisting him!?* I did all the hard work!

Duff, you're all wet!

THE CENTURION PROJECT

It was Halloween night, but this particular year it was so not about creepy, scary costumes. Both Drakken and Duff Killigan were fighting over something called the Centurion Project until I showed up and swiped it from their evil clutches. I just wanted to return it to the scientist who invented it, but it got stuck on my wrist. Next thing I know, it grew into this high-tech suit of armor. So unfashionable, but so helpful with Shego, Drakken, and Killigan all after me. This Centurion thing was really cool—I fought like I had super-powers. Blasts of hurricane-strength winds came from the arms of this suit, and before I was done, Drakken, Shego, and Killigan were disposed of like stale candy corn.

More tricks than treats

Just call me Robo-Kim.

This "costume" rocked!

THE SENIORS

Salon Ron

Don Juan Ron

Talk-too-long Ron

It all started when I told Ron to get a haircut. It was so stylin' that he became Mr. Popularity and decided he needed hair gel to maintain his new look. We trekked all the way to France to get some and found out there were rolling blackouts all over Europe. Turned out the multibillionaire Señor Senior, Senior, and his son Señor Senior, Junior, were using mega-amounts of electricity with a billion-watt tanning light. Of course, Ron had to mention that they could turn their island lair into an evil island with lasers, piranhas, and Spinning Tops of Doom. Even worse, they listened to him! Thanks, Ron.

Our next visit was not so cordial. We had to dodge lasers and some major Spinning Tops of Doom, but we managed to shut down their arsenal before they did any real damage.

CLONED

Me, me, and . . . me!

Me, letting me have it

I'll never forget the time I ended up fighting myself . . . well, sort of. Dr. Drakken got the brilliant idea to clone me and make an army of Kim Possibles. Next thing I know, I'm fighting myself! That's right, clones of yours truly! Wade got the scoop that these clones had one big weakness. They melted if you hit them with a combination of hydrogen, oxygen, and carbon dioxide—aka SODA! Sure enough, just as three K.P. clones were about to pounce, I sprayed them from a conveniently well-placed soda machine, and they melted.

Soda saved the day! I knew it wasn't all that bad for you . . . unless, of course, you are a cheap-imitation clone.

Gooped for good—aka creamed clones!

SMARTY MART

My fashion don't

Turtle trouble

Me paying for discount jeans—so not my style

I was out trying to save some manatees when I fell into the water and ripped my Club Banana pants. Since I was out in the middle of nowhere (with no pants), I ended up buying a pair of pants at— *gasp*—Smarty Mart. It just so happened that on that day, a Smarty Mart employee hit the airwaves and threatened to destroy the Internet unless everyone sent him one dollar. Ron and I ended up paying "Frugal Lucre" a visit at his oh-so-secret lair—the basement of his mom's house. He captured us in a giant net and left us dangling over snapping turtles! Escaping was no big. Problem was, capturing him meant I had to be seen—*again*—in a Smarty Mart!

Ron's big headline

Brick's uphill battle

My awesome jetpack!

Ron's brilliant idea to become a star reporter for the school paper started the whole mess. First he wrote that I was HOT for the quarterback Brick (so not true). Then we found out that the Teen Extreme TV Queen, Adrena Lynn, was a fake—she totally used a dummy in all her extreme adventures. Ron reported this, and her TV show got canceled. Sure enough, Adrena didn't take the news well. At a local amusement park, she strapped Brick (who everyone *now* thought was my boyfriend) to a runaway roller coaster, and then Ron to some twirling ride. I saved Ron and Brick just in time. Then I took Adrena Lynn for a real extreme stunt ride, à la the K.P. jetpack (I did some pretty cool flying, I must admit).

TOO COOL FOR YOU

MAGAZINE DECEMBER

POSSIBLE
VOTED ONE OF THE
TOP TEN
TRENDIEST
CRIME FIGHTERS

Entertainment Hourly
THE MAGAZINE FOR TH
WHO CAN'T WAIT A WE

**Hollywood Rumor Mill: POSSIBLE Fuming After She
Rumored to Be Hitting the Talk Show Circuit**

MIDDLETON WEEKLY WONDER

THURSDAY, OCTOBER 5

Possible's Sidekick Outwits Monkey Man

Ron Stoppable, the ever-fumbling sidekick to Middleton's own Kim Possible, outwitted an ape-man who authorities report is none other than Lord Monty Fiske (aka Monkey Fist). Stoppable used mystical monkey power to overcome the deranged Fiske in a fierce kung fu battle. Possible was unable to save the world herself due to a prior family commitment to visit her cousin Larry (the geek). She was quoted as saying, "I'm very proud of Ron." After the mission, Stoppable reportedly had an incredible craving for banana cream pie.

Better Headlines

Wisconsin Week Magazine

MIDDLETON WEEKLY WO

Teen Crime Fighter Saves State

In a heroic battle at the Wisconsin Cheese Wheel Mall, teen crime fighter Kim Possible and her side-kick Ron Stoppable thwarted the evil Dr. Drakken's plan to destroy the state of Wisconsin by flooding the state with magma. Using their razor-sharp wits (and some melted cheese), Possible and Stoppable were able to outduel Drakken's green accomplice Shego send the evil pair up a cheesy river.

Possible Protects Haughty Highness

In a daring mission, Middleton's own Kim Possible and her loyal sidekick, what's-his-name, battled a group of rogue knights at the local mini-golf course. Possible was assigned to protect Europe's Prince Wally, now known locally as "the Transfer Student Formerly Known as Prince." Golfers watched the daring Possible swing into action on the sixth hole as she dodged laser beams and battled with the poise and grace of a topflight cheerleader. After the mission, the teen crime fighter was quoted as saying, "No big." Witnesses were both impressed with Possible's prowess and miffed at the long delay while they waited to play the sixth hole. All were granted a free game, courtesy of Middleton Mini-Golf.

CHEER LEADER KIM POSSIBLE THINKS QUARTERBACK BRICK FLAGG IS H.O.T.

MIDDLETON TRIBUNE SUN-JOURNAL GAZETTE

Business News:
SMARTY MART STOCK UP 24% AFTER POSSIBLE PULLS PLUG ON BARGAIN BASEMENT CROOK

Keep those cards, letters & e-mails coming in!

Dear Kim:
I think you are the coolest crime fighter ever! You're also the cutest cheerleader ever! Send my regards to Ron, Rufus, and Wade.
Love ya,
Richie,
age 12

Kim,
You rock! You're our idol!
Signed:
Girls' Club of Middleton

Dear Kim:
Thank you for saving the world. Without the world, Santa would have no place to deliver presents at Christmas. I love you.

Sherri,
age 6

Dearest Kim:
Our deepest appreciation for helping our state withstand that evil Drakken character. You saved our cheese, and we will always be grateful. You will forever be in the hearts of all Wisconsinites—second only to the Green Bay Packers, of course.

Sincerely,
The Honorable Governor of the State of Wisconsin

Dear Kimberly Ann:
I know you're busy saving the world, going to school, and being a cheerleader and all, but you could take a few minutes to call your grandmother. I miss hearing from you.
I love you, Pookie.
Nana Possible
P.S.: If you have to go fight villains after dark, at least wear a sweater.

Kim,
If I could go back and do high school over, I'd want to be a superhero just like you! My kids (ages 3 and 5) say they want to be Kim Possible when they grow up.
Best,
Dana, age 32

Hi, Kim:
I'm a really big fan. I love the clothes you wear—I think you've got the coolest look. Maybe when you give up fighting with bad guys you could become a model or a movie actress.
So not the drama.
Jenna492
age 12

Dear K.P.:

I know it's a long way off, but if you don't have a date for your senior prom, please call me. I'd love to take you. I'm not a crime fighter, but I am on the junior-varsity football team at my high school. I wish we had cheerleaders like you. You're the coolest cheerleading crime fighter I've ever seen!

Yours always,

Nick, age 14

Hi, Kim:

I think you are so in style. You wear the coolest outfits, even when you're battling bizarre robot babes from beyond. Love your hair. Don't cut it—it's so the look!

Best,

FashionGirl99, age 12

Hi, Kim:

Hope it works out between you and Josh (I think he's cute). Do you think he'll ask you to the next school dance? I hope he does, for your sake. But if he doesn't, it's his loss. You're my hero.

Pam, age 11

Kim:
You are my favorite hero—NOT!
Shego,
   age: none of your business

Kim:
You are totally awesome. I was really scared when you were fighting those knights at the golf course, but as usual, you came through. I think you could defeat any criminal in the world.
You're the best!
Dina, age 12

Hi, Kim;
I really like the super gadgets you use when you're fighting crooks. Where do you get all that cool stuff? Can I order any of it from the Internet?
Regards, Eric, age 8

Dear Kim:
I think it is really cool how you use all your gadgets and locate the crooks' hideouts. I also think it's cool how you save the world and fight Shego.
Great job!
Rebecca, age 10

Kim,
I know we don't say it often, but we're very proud of you. You're a top student, excellent cheerleader, and a good little crime fighter. We love you.
Mom & Dad

KIM IN ACTION

Drakken finds the nastiest toys.

Fighting with Monkey Fist

Three against one is _so_ not fair.

Me and Shego fighting. She's the green one.
Wouldn't her jacket look way better on me?